MOLLY'S
SPECIAL WISH

Written by Robyn Supraner
Illustrated by Margot Rocklen

Troll Associates

Library of Congress Cataloging in Publication Data

Supraner, Robyn.
    Molly's special wish.

    Summary: Concerned that her friend the moon will not be
able to find her after she moves to a distant town, Molly
takes the moon with her in a box.
    [1. Moving, Household—Fiction. 2. Moon—Fiction]
I. Rocklen, Margot, ill.   II. Title.
PZ7.S9652Mo   1986   [E]   85-14087
ISBN 0-8167-0660-3 (lib. bdg.)
ISBN 0-8167-0661-1 (pbk.)

MOLLY'S
SPECIAL WISH

Molly was moving. She was
moving to a different city, to a
different house, far away from
Elm Street.

It was the last day for digging
worms with Cynthia. It was the
last day for swinging in the
hammock. It was the last day
for cooling off under the hose.
It was the last day for teasing
Jimmy Brown. Tomorrow,
things would be different.

At lunch time, Molly sat at
the table and looked out the
window.
"This is my last lunch by this
window, in this kitchen,"
she said.

She nibbled at her sandwich.
It was tuna fish, her favorite.
Today it tasted terrible.

She fed some ant eggs to Goldie
the goldfish.

"I hope you're not the only fish in the city," she said. "I hope you find a friend."

Goldie swished her tail. She made two bubbles. She didn't seem worried at all.

That night Molly said to her
mother, "This is my last bath in
this bathtub, in this bathroom."
She said to her father, "This is
my last night in a bedroom with
sunflowers on the walls."

Her mother and father kissed
her. They told her she would
love their new home. They told
her she would make a lot of
friends. They told her Cynthia
could come and visit. Then they
told her that they loved her and
said good night.

Molly looked around her room.
Things were different already.
Her toys were packed in cartons.
Her closet was empty. Even her
curtains were gone.

Molly could see the moon. Each
night it came to her window.
Sometimes it was thin as an
apple slice. Sometimes, like
tonight, it was fat. Cynthia
liked to wish on the first star.
She said it was lucky. But Molly
always wished on the moon.

16

Tonight she was worried. Could the moon follow her? Would it know where to find her on the sixth floor of an apartment house? Would it know which window was hers?

"Hi, moon," she whispered. "It's Molly. I won't be here tomorrow. I'm moving to somewhere far away."

Then she shut her eyes and
made a wish.

When she opened her eyes, the
moon was smiling. Molly was
smiling, too.

That night, before she went to
sleep, Molly left an empty box
on her windowsill.

The next morning, the moon
was gone. The sun was starting
to climb high in the sky. Molly
covered the box with a lid.

Then she dressed in her moving-
day clothes and went to see about
breakfast.

"What's in the box?" asked her
mother.

"The moon," said Molly. "I've
got the moon."

"That's silly," said her father.
"You can't put the moon in a
box."

"I didn't *put* it in," said Molly.
"It *went* in by itself."
"The car is jam-packed," said
her father. "We don't have room
for the moon."

25

"Don't worry," said Molly. "I'll
hold it on my lap."
She finished her toast in three
big bites and guzzled the last of
her milk.
Her father said, "Eat slowly!"
Her mother said, "Don't gulp!"
But Molly didn't hear them. She
and the moon box were gone.

The movers came at eight
o'clock. They emptied Molly's
house. The walls looked sad.
There were white spots where
the pictures used to hang. They
looked like lonely ghosts.

Cynthia came over.
"What's in the box?" she asked.
"The moon," said Molly. "I'm
taking it with me."

"You're kidding," said Cynthia.
"Let me look inside."
Molly opened the box.

"It's empty," said Cynthia. "I
don't see a thing."
"Of course not," said Molly.
"You can't see the moon in the
daytime. It's invisible."
"Time to go," said Molly's
mother. "It's time to say good-
bye."

Cynthia gave Molly her lucky
peach pit. Molly gave Cynthia
her lucky baseball cap. They
hugged and kissed and promised
to write every day.

"Time to go!" called Molly's
father. Molly climbed into the
car. The trip took six hours,
counting a stop for lunch.

32

Everywhere Molly went, the
moon box went, too.

At last they came to Queen
Street. The houses were very
tall. They stood shoulder to
shoulder, like red brick giants.
The trees had little fences all
around. Inside the fences,
someone had planted marigolds
and petunias.

Molly and her parents took the
elevator to the sixth floor. They
found apartment 602.

36

The moving men were there.
Molly's father showed them
where to put the furniture. The
green couch looked funny. It
looked like it missed Elm Street.

Molly's mother put the dishes
away. She put away the knives
and forks and spoons. She put
the napkins in a drawer. She put
the glasses on a shelf. Then she
opened a brown paper package.

Inside were flowers, picked from
the garden on Elm Street. There
were roses and daisies and blue
forget-me-nots.

Molly smelled the roses.
"Aren't they lovely!" said her
mother. "You'll see. Tomorrow
things will look even better."
"Maybe," said Molly.
"Maybe?" her mother asked.
"It depends," said Molly. "It
depends on the moon."

For supper, there was a picnic
on the living-room floor—cold
chicken and rolls and tomatoes.
Suddenly, Molly jumped to her
feet.
"Oh, no!" she yelped. "The
moon! I forgot to let out the
moon!"
"It's summer," said her father.
"It's too early for the moon."

Molly raced to her bedroom.
She put the moon box on her
windowsill and slowly raised the
lid. Then she opened the
window.

"Poor old moon," she
whispered, "stuck in a box all
day."

That night, after she had been
hugged and kissed and tucked
into bed, Molly waited for the
moon. She waited and waited
and waited.

"Please come, moon," she
whispered. "Please."

But still the moon didn't come.
Molly could see a few stars. She
could see the pale sky. She could
see the red lights of a passing
plane.
"Come on, moon," said Molly.

And then, peeping over her
windowsill, fat and mellow and
beautifully round, it came. The
moon. It rose up into the sky,
higher and higher. Then it
smiled, its wonderful silvery
smile, right at Molly.
And Molly smiled back.